Today, Sarah is tucked up in bed under her blanket. She's feeling a bit poorly . . .

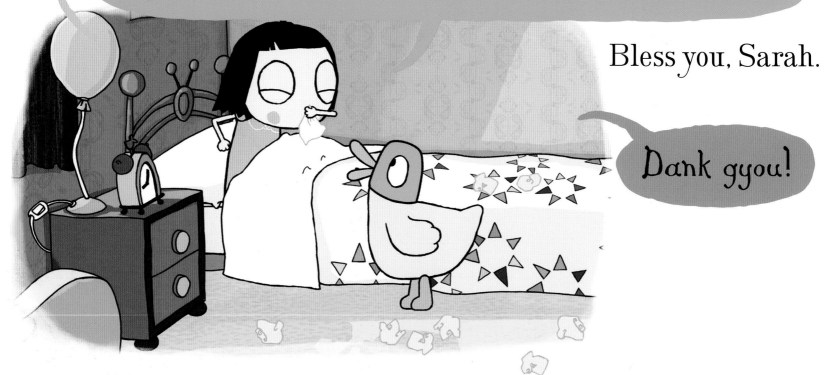

Quack! says Duck, waking Sarah up.

Hello, Du . . . u . . . u . . . . . . uck-choo!

Bless you, Sarah.

Dank gyou!

It sounds like Sarah has a cold, Duck.

Aaaa-actchoo!

Quack!

Poor Sarah.

Duck puts Sarah's hat on and tries doing a little dance
to cheer her up.

Heheh! Danks for drying
to dear me up, Duck.
Sniff, sniff. Aaaa-choo!

Sarah makes her way into the kitchen. Ah, good idea, Sarah, some honey and lemon water. That should make you feel better.

Want some, Duck?

says Sarah.

Quack!

Duck takes a sip.

Ack-agg! . . . Cough!

Oh dear, it doesn't look like Duck likes it very much.

Sarah likes the honey and lemon water, but she still can't stop sneezing. Perhaps she needs a trip to the doctor.

Sarah wraps up
nice and warm,

and the pair head
out to the doctor's.

Sarah and Duck arrive at the doctor's and make their way to the reception desk.

Hello, dear. What's your name? asks the receptionist.

Sarah . . .

sniffs Sarah.

OK. Take a seat, Sarah. The doctor will see you shortly.

Quack.

Poor Sarah. She's really not feeling very well at all.

Great idea, Duck. A magazine will help to take Sarah's mind off her cold.

Dank you, Dug.

Duck peeks over the top of the magazine to see if it's working.

That dress suits you, Duck!

Heheh! giggles Sarah.

Duck makes a good giraffe too.

Funny Duck!

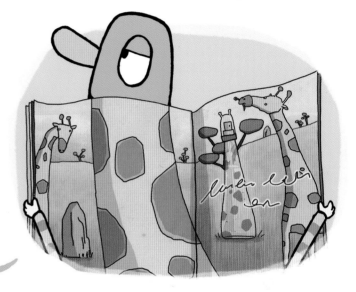

Now he wants to be a ballet dancer!

Ha, ha, ha . . . a . . . a . . . choo!

sneezes Sarah.

The doctor is ready to see you now, Sarah.

says the receptionist.

Duck looks around
for something to do
while he waits.

Well, that playhouse certainly
looks like a lot of fun.

Afternoon, Duck!

Quack.

I wonder where this
crocodile goes . . .

Duck zooms down the crocodile slide and . . .

. . . straight into a pile of toys!

Quack.

plink!

plink!

What was that noise?

Quack, plink!

Quack, plonk!

Quack, plink!

Oh! It's a toy piano . . . and that sounds just
like Sarah's favourite song, Duck!

It looks like Duck has an idea.

Duck nudges the slide to the doctor's door.
I wonder what he's doing ...

plink!

plink!

Where are you going, Duck? Duck?

Look, Sarah! Duck has left you a surprise.

Oh. Funny Duck.

Sarah climbs up the crocodile and slides down . . .

... all the way to the front door! What's going on here then?

Sarah hums along to the musical ducks.

Mmmm, mmmm.

Mmmm, mmm.

Thank you, Duck.

Good work, chaps. It sounds like Sarah is feeling a lot better.

Oh no. It sounds like Duck's caught your cold, Sarah . . .

The End